MYSTERIES

THE
ESCAPE FROM
MYSTERY
ISLAND

by Michael Anthony Steele
illustrated by Dario Brizuela

Batman created by Bob Kane with Bill Finger

STONE ARCH BOOKS
a capstone imprint

Published by Stone Arch Books,
an imprint of Capstone.
1710 Roe Crest Drive
North Mankato, Minnesota 56003
capstonepub.com

Library of Congress Cataloging-in-Publication Data
Names: Steele, Michael Anthony, author. |
Brizuela, Dario. illustrator.
Title: The escape from Mystery Island / by Michael Anthony
Steele; illustrated by Dario Brizuela.
Description: North Mankato, Minnesota : Stone Arch Books, an
imprint of Capstone, [2021] | Series: Batman and Scooby-Doo!
mysteries | "Batman created by Bob Kane with Bill Finger" |
Audience: Ages 8–11. | Audience: Grades 4–6 . | Summary: When
an uncharted island springs up in Gotham City Harbor, Batman
and Mystery Inc. join forces to uncover who created the tropical
paradise, but soon find themselves under attack by a host of vile
vegetation and prehistoric plants.
Identifiers: LCCN 2021002508 (print) | LCCN 2021002509 (ebook) |
ISBN 9781663910462 (hardcover) | ISBN 9781663920218
(paperback) | ISBN 9781663910431 (ebook pdf)
Subjects: CYAC: Superheroes—Fiction. | Islands—Fiction. |
Plants—Fiction. | Mystery and detective stories. | Fantasy.
Classification: LCC PZ7.S8147 Esm 2021 (print) | LCC PZ7.S8147
(ebook) | DDC [Fic]—dc23
LC record available at https://lccn.loc.gov/2021002508
LC ebook record available at https://lccn.loc.gov/2021002509

Designer: Tracy Davies

Printed and bound in China. PO4911

TABLE OF CONTENTS

MEeT BATMAN AND

BATMAN

While still a boy, Bruce Wayne watched his parents die at the hands of a petty criminal. After that tragic day, the young billionaire vowed to rid Gotham City of evil and keep its people safe. To achieve this goal, he trained his mind and body to become the World's Greatest Detective. Donning a costume inspired by a fearful run-in with bats at a young age, the Dark Knight now aims to strike the same sense of fear in his foes. But the Caped Crusader doesn't always work alone. He often teams up with other crime fighters, including Robin, Batgirl, Batwing, Batwoman, and even . . . Mystery Inc.

THE MYSTERY INC. GANG

Traveling in a van named the Mystery Machine, these meddling kids, and their crime-fighting canine, solve mysteries all over the country—even in Gotham City!

THE
MYSTERY INC. GANG

Scooby-Doo

A happy hound with a super snout, Scooby-Doo is the mascot of Mystery Inc. He'll do anything for a Scooby Snack!

Shaggy Rogers

Shaggy is a laid-back dude who would rather search for food than clues . . . but he usually finds both!

Fred Jones, Jr.

Fred is the oldest member of the group. Friendly and fun-loving, he's a good sport—and good at them too.

Velma Dinkley

Velma is clever and book smart. She may be the youngest member of the team, but she's an old pro at cracking cases.

Daphne Blake

Brainy and bold, the fashion-forward Daphne solves mysteries with street smarts and a sense of style.

CHAPTER 1

THE BIG CATCH

Ploop!

Shaggy dropped his fishing line into the water. "Like, this will be the one. I just know it," he said with a grin. "Fish dinner tonight!"

The Mystery Inc. gang enjoyed a day off aboard a boat floating out in Gotham City Harbor. The calls of seagulls filled the salty air as they each fished over the side.

WHIP-FZZZZZ! Daphne cast her line into the water.

"What a great way to spend the afternoon," she said.

Klik-klik-klik-klik-klik-klik.

Velma slowly cranked her reel. "Be sure to thank your friend for the use of his boat, Fred." She pulled her lure out of the water before casting it out again. "It's too bad the fish aren't biting today."

Fred laughed. "Well, Terry said we could use his boat as long as we needed." He pulled up an empty lure too. "Maybe it'll be long enough to finally catch something."

Daphne jutted a thumb over her shoulder. "Then there will be some excitement to keep Scooby awake."

ZZZZZZZZZZZ . . .

Scooby-Doo was kicked back in a deck chair, sound asleep. He cradled his fishing pole in his arms.

Suddenly, his rod jerked beneath his paws. Scooby startled awake as his pole bent in front of him.

"A rish!" Scooby-Doo shouted. "I raught a rish!" He cranked the reel as fast as he could.

Fred, Daphne, and Velma set their poles down and joined him.

"Way to go, Scooby," Fred said.

"Let's help him reel it in!" Daphne added.

Meanwhile, on the opposite side of the boat, Shaggy's rod jerked and bent toward the water.

"Like, I raught a rish . . ." Shaggy shook his head. "I mean . . . I caught a fish too!"

Everyone was so busy helping Scooby-Doo, they didn't see Shaggy struggling with his pole.

"Uh, gang?" Shaggy put both feet on the deck railing as he struggled to crank his reel. "This feels like a big one!"

On the other side of the boat, everyone held tight to Scooby-Doo's pole.

"On the count of three," Fred said. "One . . . two . . . three!"

As the group pulled on Scooby's fishing rod, Shaggy was dragged over the side of the boat.

SPLOOSH!

No one noticed the splash as they excitedly helped Scooby reel in his catch. Scooby-Doo cranked faster as he pulled back on his pole. After a bit, another fishing rod rose out of the water . . . with Shaggy holding tight! He was covered with seaweed and an octopus sat atop his head.

"Ruh-roh," Scooby said before giggling.

Everyone else joined in the laughter.

Velma put her hands on her hips. "Quit fooling around, Shaggy."

Shaggy spit out a stream of water as the annoyed sea creature slid off his head and plopped back into the water. "Like, I think mine got away."

Daphne pointed toward Shaggy. "What's that?" she asked.

"I think it's just seaweed," Shaggy said, pulling a slimy, green strand from his shoulder.

"Not that, Shaggy." Daphne shook her head. "Behind you."

She pointed at the huge mound of vegetation poking out of the water. It was a large island that none of them had noticed while they fished.

"That's strange," Velma said. "There aren't supposed to be any islands on this side of Gotham City Harbor."

"Looks like we have another mystery on our hands," Fred added. "Let's check it out."

Shaggy climbed into the boat and toweled off. "Like, I thought we were taking a break from mysteries today," he said.

Velma shrugged. "Well, sometimes the mysteries find us."

While Shaggy changed into some dry clothes, Fred piloted the boat toward the island. Once the boat was tied off, everyone hopped out and trudged across the beach.

Velma led the way as they moved deeper into the thick jungle. They made their way past giant ferns and ducked under huge leaves and thick vines.

"This is amazing," Velma said. "These types of plants shouldn't be able to grow this far north, right next to Gotham City."

Shaggy and Scooby-Doo brought up the rear as the group moved through the dense vegetation.

"Like, is it just me?" Shaggy asked. "Or is this place getting creepier the deeper we go?"

Scooby shook his head. "Rit's not just you. Rit's very creepy."

As Shaggy moved forward, a vine dropped from above and slithered around his waist. "That tickles, Scoob," Shaggy said with a giggle. He brushed away the vine without looking at it. "I know you're scared, pal, but keep your tail to yourself."

Scooby-Doo whimpered. "Rat wasn't me," he replied, pointing up at the treetops. "Rook!"

"Zoinks!" Shaggy shouted as another vine shot toward him. He ducked as it struck at him like a giant snake.

Scooby-Doo leaped off the ground as two vines tried to snare his legs.

Shaggy and Scooby ran to catch up with the others. They dodged more vines along the way.

"Like, look out!" Shaggy warned. "The plants are attacking!"

"Come on, Shaggy," Daphne said with a dismissive wave. "Plants don't attack people."

Just then, several vines shot down from the treetops and coiled around Fred, Daphne, and Velma. They plucked the three of them off the ground.

"Usually," Daphne added as the vine tightened around her body.

"Like, feet don't fail me now!" Shaggy shouted as he ran away.

"Rait for me!" Scooby shouted as he sprinted after his friend.

The two ducked under more vicious vines as they ran back the way they had come. They were almost to the beach when snake-like vines snared both of them. They hung upside down, wrapped tight in the green coils.

Just then, a dark figure soared through the treetops above them.

Shaggy shivered as the shape drew closer and closer. "Like, I guess this is how it ends. Huh, pal?"

Scooby-Doo's teeth chattered in fear. "I can't rook," he said, squeezing his eyes shut.

"Oh, boy," Shaggy said. "Me neither." He closed his eyes too.

WHIP-WHIP!

The dark figure threw two objects toward the bound buddies. The sharp items cut through the vines, and Shaggy and Scooby fell to the ground.

THUD! THUD!

Free from the vines, Shaggy and Scooby-Doo hugged each other. They trembled as they kept their eyes shut tight.

Suddenly, the two friends heard something land on the jungle floor and then slowly walk toward them. They began to whimper.

"You can both open your eyes now," said a deep voice.

Shaggy and Scooby each opened one eye to take a peek. A masked figure stood before them. He wore a grim expression and a long, black cape.

Shaggy's eyes widened. "Batman!"

CHAPTER 2

NO ESCAPE

Shaggy and Scooby-Doo led Batman to their trapped friends. With a flick of the wrist, the Dark Knight sent three more Batarangs flying.

WHIP-WHIP-WHIP!

The small, bat-shaped weapons sliced through the air and then through the vines holding Fred, Daphne, and Velma.

THUD-THUD! THUD!

They fell to the ground and shook off the now lifeless vines.

"Thanks, Batman!" Fred said as he got to his feet.

Daphne dusted off her dress. "What are you doing here?" she asked.

"I'm guessing the same as you," Batman replied. "Investigating an island that has no business being this close to Gotham City."

Velma touched an enormous leaf. "And these plants have no business being in our own time period," she added. "Some of them look prehistoric, like plants from the dinosaur age."

Batman marched forward and examined the leaf. "I think you're right."

"Hold the phone!" Fred said. "Daphne, didn't you tell us about a news story you read recently? Something about a burglary at the Gotham City Natural History Museum?"

"That's right," Daphne said. "And the only things stolen were a bunch of fossilized seeds."

Velma gasped. "I think that's a clue, Batman."

The hero nodded. "I agree." He marched deeper into the jungle. "Stay close," he ordered. "And don't touch any of the plants."

Shaggy laughed nervously. "Like, can you tell the plants not to touch *us*?"

"Reah," agreed Scooby-Doo.

The gang followed Batman along a narrow trail in the jungle. They passed many strange and oversized plants. But none were as strange as the plants surrounding a small clearing. They had thick stalks holding up open mouths shaped like clamshells. Rows of sharp thorns lined their mouths like teeth.

"Jinkies," Velma said, pointing at the huge plants. "Those look like giant Venus flytraps."

"Whoa!" Fred said. "They're the plants that catch flies and other insects that land on them."

Shaggy glanced around. "If the plants are that big, I'd hate to see the size of the flies."

Scooby-Doo whimpered as he stayed close to Shaggy.

"Stay clear of them," Batman ordered. "They shouldn't harm you if you don't touch them."

As soon as the words were out of his mouth, the nearest giant flytrap lunged at the Dark Knight. It scooped him off his feet and slammed its mouth tight around him. Batman was trapped inside.

"Jeepers!" Daphne said. "What do we do?"

TZZZZZZ!

Electricity danced over the outside of the plant. The large flytrap began to smoke before it sprang back open. Electricity sparked from Batman's gloves as he stepped out of the open mouth. The killer plant smoked some more before it wilted behind him.

SNAP! SNAP-SNAP-SNAP!

The rest of the flytraps hungrily snapped at the others. Everyone gathered in the center of the clearing.

TZZZZZZ! Batman shocked one of the plants with his electrified gloves. As it wilted to the ground, the crime fighter hurled a net at another huge flytrap. The net wrapped around its snapping jaws before it could catch Fred.

WHIP! WHIP! The Dark Knight sent two sets of bolas flying toward two more monster plants. The heavy balls at the end of long ropes wrapped around their jaws before the plants could chomp down on Daphne and Velma.

"Ruh-roh!" Scooby-Doo shouted as one of the plants grabbed his tail. It dragged him closer to the snapping jaws of the other plants.

"Oh, no!" Velma said. "It has Scooby-Doo!"

Shaggy grabbed a stick. "Like, fetch, Scoob!" He hurled the stick toward his friend.

Scooby caught the long stick in his mouth just as one of the plants chomped down on him. The stick kept the plant's mouth open while Scooby scrambled clear.

"Ranks, Raggy," Scooby said as he joined everyone in the center of the clearing.

"You kids need to get off this island," Batman said. "It's too dangerous."

"Like, you don't have to tell me twice," Shaggy said as he bolted out of the clearing.

"Reah!" agreed Scooby as he tore after him.

The rest of the gang followed as they sprinted down the trail, back the way they had come. They ran past more attacking vines, ducking and dodging along the way. They didn't look back as they sped through the thick jungle.

"Like, I'm ready to be off this crazy island and safely aboard our boat," Shaggy said as he ran. "With all the snacks!"

"Re too!" Scooby agreed.

The gang ran and ran, but all they saw was more jungle. The beach was nowhere in sight.

"I don't understand," Velma said between breaths. "We should have arrived at the beach by now."

"Do you think we took a wrong turn?" Fred asked as he caught up to her.

Shaggy skidded to a stop. "Like, I don't think so." He pointed to the treetops. "Look!"

The rest of the gang stopped and followed Shaggy's finger. He pointed to their boat high above them, nestled in a treetop.

"How did the boat get way up there?" Daphne asked.

"Wait a minute," Fred said. "What's that next to it?"

Another vehicle rested atop a nearby tree. It was long, sleek, and completely black. A long, sharp fin jutted out above a jet engine in the back.

"That's the Batboat," Velma explained. "Do you know what this means?"

"That we're going to have to climb a tree to get to our snacks?" Shaggy asked.

Velma shook her head. "It means the island is getting bigger," she replied. "And we're completely trapped."

Both Shaggy and Scooby-Doo gulped loudly.

CHAPTER 3

FLOWER POWER

"We have to tell Batman about this," Fred said.

Velma nodded. "I agree."

Shaggy fidgeted nervously. "Like, maybe Scoob and I should stay and watch the boat," he suggested.

Scooby-Doo nodded vigorously. "Reah! Reah!"

Daphne glanced up at the tree. "I don't think it's going anywhere, guys."

"I was afraid you were going to say that," Shaggy said with a nervous laugh.

With Shaggy and Scooby-Doo bringing up the rear, the gang marched back through the jungle. They watched for snake-like vines, but no more of them attacked. When they reached the giant flytraps, the monster plants were either wilted or still tied up with Batman's weapons. The gang pressed on, deeper into the jungle.

They followed the thin trail until it opened up into a field of enormous pink flowers. The gang snaked their way through the colorful vegetation.

"Wow," Daphne said. "I've never seen flowers like these."

She leaned over one to get a better look. As her face neared, the flower began to tremble. Daphne took a step back just before the plant attacked.

FFT! FFT-FFT!

"Jeepers!" Daphne shouted. She barely ducked out of the way as the flower shot several sharp darts toward her. She put her hands on her hips. "Well, that's just rude."

Suddenly, *all* the flowers began to tremble.

FFT! FFT-FFT! FFT-FFT! FFT! FFT!

The rest of the flowers launched darts at the Mystery Inc. gang. They ducked and dodged as sharp missiles flew in from all sides.

"Zoinks!" Shaggy shouted as he leaped into the air. He twisted and turned his body in every direction. Each time he moved, the darts narrowly missed him.

Scooby-Doo whimpered as he dodged deadly darts alongside his friend. He ducked and jerked along with Shaggy as if they were doing some crazy dance.

"Let's get out of here!" Fred shouted as they all fled the field of fierce flowers.

Everyone sprinted into the jungle and continued down the narrow path. They traveled deeper and deeper into the island, but they still hadn't caught up to the Dark Knight.

Shaggy glanced around. "Like, yoo-hoo! Mister Batman, sir?" He shivered. "Can you come out before any more plants try to eat, strangle, or puncture us?"

"Reah," Scooby agreed. "A rittle help."

The gang trudged farther down the trail, but there was no sign of the crime fighter anywhere.

BAM! POW! BAM! A commotion up ahead caught their attention.

"What was that?" Daphne asked.

Velma took the lead. "I think we finally found Batman," she said.

Everyone poured on the speed until they made it to another clearing. The gang peeked through the leaves to see the strangest thing. Batman fought off two trees! Except they were more like tree people.

The creatures had thick, trunk-like bodies and walked around with bare roots for feet. They swiped at the Super Hero with long, crooked branches for arms and scowled at him with faces on giant flowers.

Batman flipped backward, dodging the attack. Then he landed a flying kick on one of the trees.

BAM! The Dark Knight knocked the tree monster back into the jungle. The other tree creature came up from behind, wrapping its branches around him. The crime fighter bent forward, lifting the tree off the ground. Then he grabbed one of the branches and flipped it over his shoulder.

WHOOP!

The second tree monster flew into the dense vegetation.

The Mystery Inc. gang ran into the clearing to join him.

"What were those things?" Fred asked.

"I thought I told you to get to safety," Batman said.

"We tried," Daphne explained. "But the island is growing, and now our boat is stuck up a tree."

"No one is going anywhere," said a woman's voice.

WHIP! With lightning speed, a thorny vine shot out of nowhere and wrapped around Batman. It pinned his arms to his body as it lifted him off the ground. The hero grunted as he struggled to break free, but it was no use.

Another vine lowered into view. This one carried a woman with red hair, greenish skin, and a sinister grin.

"Jinkies!" Velma pointed up at the woman. "It's Gotham City Super-Villain Pamela Isley," she said. "Better known as Poison Ivy."

Shaggy and Scooby-Doo gulped as they slowly backed into the jungle. Just as they did, ten tree monsters stepped into the clearing. Three of them grabbed Fred, Velma, and Daphne. They didn't spot Shaggy or Scooby.

Poison Ivy cackled with laughter as Shaggy and Scooby-Doo hugged each other in fear.

"Like, what are we going to do, Scoob?" Shaggy asked in a whisper.

Scooby-Doo whimpered and shook his head. "I ron't know."

CHAPTER 4

UNDERCOVER

Fred, Daphne, and Velma struggled as the tree people carried them closer to Poison Ivy. The vine holding the crime fighter moved him closer as well. He grunted as he struggled, but he couldn't break free.

"I'm not surprised to see you here, Batman," the villain said. "But I wasn't expecting a group of meddling kids."

"Let me guess," Velma said. "You're the one who stole the fossilized seeds from the museum."

Poison Ivy laughed. "That's right," she said. "You see, only I can . . ."

". . . make them grow using your power over plants," Velma finished. "You're probably using their roots to pull up soil from the ocean floor, creating the island."

"That's . . . right," Ivy said, cocking her head at Velma. "An expanding island that . . ."

". . . that will first take over Gotham City and then the world," Velma interrupted again.

Ivy sighed. "And prehistoric plants and humans . . . ," she began.

". . . can't live together," Velma finished. She rolled her eyes. "But that's probably what you want since people have been so rotten to plants in the first place."

"Velma," Fred whispered. "Don't interrupt villains in the middle of their speeches about their evil plans."

"Yeah," Daphne agreed. "It makes them crankier than usual."

"Let them go, Ivy," Batman ordered.

"Now, why would I do that?" Poison Ivy asked. "They would miss the show." She raised a hand and three vines shot down from the treetops.

WHIP-WHIP-WHIP! Each of them wrapped around Velma, Fred, and Daphne. The gang struggled to get loose as the vines lifted them high off the ground.

Ivy raised both hands and the ground began to shake.

RUMMMMMMBLE!

Roots burst from the soil and snaked around each other. More and more emerged, creating tangled walls as passageways. By the time the ground quit shaking, a huge maze of vegetation was laid out before them.

"Now, let's see how long you last in my maze, Batman," Ivy said as the Dark Knight was lowered closer to the ground. The villain snapped her fingers. "Oh, I almost forgot." She nodded at one of the tree monsters and it marched forward. It reached out with a crooked branch and yanked off Batman's Utility Belt.

"There you go," Ivy said. "No cheating."

Poison Ivy laughed as the vine dropped the Dark Knight into the center of the maze.

Shaggy and Scooby-Doo watched from the bushes as a line of tree people marched into the maze entrance.

BAM! BAP! BOFF!

From the sound of things, Batman was fighting them off. But more of the creatures continued to rush into the maze after him.

"Like, look at all those tree monsters," Shaggy whispered. "It's a good thing one of them hasn't spotted us yet."

Scooby-Doo didn't say anything.

"Scoob?" Shaggy asked, looking around. When he finally spotted him, the dog was crawling into a hollow log.

"Great idea, pal," Shaggy said, shuffling closer. "We'll find a place to hide until this whole thing works itself out."

To Shaggy's surprise, Scooby stood up on his hind legs, wearing the log around his waist. He poked his arms out from two knot holes and plucked the head off of a giant flower. Scooby pushed his nose through the back of the flower until his face was surrounded by large petals.

Shaggy laughed nervously. "Like, tell me you're not thinking what I think you're thinking," he said.

Scooby-Doo grabbed two crooked branches off the ground. He waved them around like long arms. "Rook, Raggy," Scooby said. "I'm a tree ronster."

Shaggy gulped. "I told you not to tell me."

Before long, Shaggy found his own hollow log, flower, and tree branches. Once he had dressed the part, he shambled over to his friend.

"Okay," Shaggy said. "Like, now what?"

"Rook," Scooby said. He pointed to one of the tree monsters. The creature in question held Batman's Utility Belt.

Shaggy gulped as he and Scooby-Doo shuffled out of hiding. They blended in with the other tree people, slowly making their way toward the one holding the Utility Belt.

"Like, I can hold that for you," Shaggy said in a deep voice. "If you want to take a turn against Batman."

The tree monster scowled at Shaggy and Scooby, looking them up and down. Shaggy began to tremble and a couple of petals fell from his head. Then the creature shoved the belt into Shaggy's arms before running into the maze with the others.

Shaggy breathed a sigh of relief. "I can't believe that worked, pal," he whispered. "Now what?"

Scooby didn't answer. Instead, his tree trunk bumped against Shaggy's.

BONK!

"What's the big idea, Scoob?" Shaggy asked.

Scooby shook his head. "It rasn't me, Raggy."

Shaggy turned to see a long line of tree monsters right behind him and Scooby-Doo. The one behind Scooby shoved him forward, making him bump into Shaggy again.

BONK!

The tree monsters pushed the two friends closer and closer to the maze entrance. Shaggy spun around and extended one of his branch arms ahead of him.

"Like, why don't you guys go ahead of us," he said. "We'll sit this one out."

"Reah!" Scooby nodded in agreement. Some of his petals fell from his head.

One of the tree monsters lumbered forward and looked the friends up and down. Then it plucked the flower from around Scooby's head. It snarled as it moved in.

"I think the jig is up, pal," Shaggy said. "Run!"

Shaggy and Scooby-Doo dropped their branches and ran into the maze. A herd of tree monsters thundered after them.

The two friends darted around corners and sprinted up passageways. They became so turned around in the complicated maze that sometimes the creatures chased them and other times they chased the tree monsters. Finally, they ducked around a corner and waited as the group of angry monsters rumbled past.

"Like, we have to get out of here and help the others," Shaggy said.

"Great idea!" Scooby said. Then he scratched his head. "How?"

Shaggy and Scooby tiptoed through the maze, carefully avoiding more tree monsters. Then they heard a loud commotion.

BAM! BOFF! BAP!

The two friends turned a corner to see the Dark Knight fighting off tree monsters. The hero landed a spinning kick on one of the creature's thick trunks, knocking it back into two others.

Then Batman blocked a blow from another tree before landing several punches, knocking it to the ground.

Once the crime fighter had taken care of the wave of tree monsters, Shaggy and Scooby ran out of hiding and straight to Batman. Unfortunately, the hero thought they were more tree monsters. He raised a fist, ready to attack.

Shaggy skidded to a stop, and Scooby rammed into him from behind.

BONK!

"Wait!" Shaggy shouted, raising his hands. "It's us! It's us!" He took off his tree disguise.

"Raggy and Rooby," Scooby added as he slipped out of his log.

"What are you doing here?" Batman asked.

"Like, we have your Utility Belt," Shaggy replied.

Shaggy handed Batman the Utility Belt just as more tree monsters appeared. The Dark Knight strapped on the belt and pulled out his grapnel.

POP!

The crime fighter shot his grapnel toward the treetops, and it hooked on a large branch. Then Batman grabbed Shaggy and Scooby as the thin cable hoisted them out of the giant maze.

"Hee-hee-hee-hee-hee-hee!" Scooby giggled as they flew to safety.

Batman let go of Shaggy and Scooby as he lightly touched down just outside the maze.

GRRRR! Poison Ivy growled in frustration.

"That does it!" she shouted. The villain closed her eyes and raised both hands, summoning all of her powers.

FWOOOSH!

The roots from the maze ripped from the ground and rocketed toward her. The remaining tree monsters ran forward, and the jungle was alive with vines snaking closer. The mass of vegetation came together to form an enormous structure around Poison Ivy.

"Jeepers," Daphne said, still suspended by her own vine. "What's happening?"

"I don't know," Velma replied as she hung beside her. "But it doesn't look good."

"I'll tell you what it looks like," Fred said. "It looks like . . . a giant spider!"

As the dust cleared, Poison Ivy rode atop a humongous spider made completely out of plants.

Shaggy gulped. "Like, I really hate spiders."

Scooby-Doo shivered beside him. "Re too!"

CHAPTER 5

BAT VS. SPIDER

FOOM!

Batman barely leaped clear as one of the spider's legs slammed toward him. The ground shook and dirt flew everywhere as it struck. The Dark Knight tucked and rolled before scrambling to his feet. He had just enough time to dodge another spider attack.

WHIP-WHIP-WHIP! The Caped Crusader's hand was a blur as he flung three special Batarangs at the creature.

Tiny red lights flashed on the Batarangs as they struck three of the spider's legs. The lights blinked faster and faster.

BOOM-BOOM! BOOM!

Branches and splinters flew everywhere as the Batarangs exploded. The giant spider stumbled, but more vines and roots twirled around its damaged legs. In no time, they were repaired completely.

Poison Ivy laughed. "We can do this all day, Batman," she said. "I have the patience of a redwood."

While Poison Ivy battled Batman, Shaggy and Scooby-Doo ran over to help their friends. Scooby stood on his hind legs while Shaggy climbed up onto his shoulders. The dog shuffled closer to Daphne so Shaggy could reach her.

"Thanks," Daphne said as Shaggy quickly unwrapped the vines from around her.

Scooby stumbled over to Fred and then to Velma. His legs wobbled under the weight.

"Almost there, Scoob," Shaggy said as he finished unwrapping Velma.

"Ruh-roh," Scooby said as his legs finally gave out.

"Whoa!" Velma shouted as she and Shaggy fell onto Scooby.

"Great job, buddy," Shaggy said as he got to his feet. He chuckled. "I always knew you were the one carrying our friendship."

Scooby-Doo rubbed his head. "Yeah, right."

Fred pointed at Batman. "Look!"

POP! The Dark Knight fired his grapnel at one of the spider's legs. Once it was locked in place, he jerked the line, ripping the leg off the plant spider. Poison Ivy laughed as a new leg grew back in its place.

"How is he going to stop her?" Fred asked.

Daphne ran toward the hero. "Maybe we can help."

Fred, Velma, and Scooby took off after her.

Shaggy crossed his arms. "Like, no way. Giant plant spiders and I don't mix."

POP! Batman fired his grapnel again and ripped off another plant leg. It flew through the air, nearly landing on Shaggy.

THUNK!

"On second thought . . ." Shaggy sprinted toward the others. "Maybe it's safer behind the Super Hero."

The Mystery Inc. gang hid behind a large tree while Batman fought off more attacks.

"How can we help, Batman?" Daphne asked.

The Dark Knight removed a small, gray canister from his Utility Belt.

"This is knock-out gas," the hero said. "If I can get it close to Ivy . . ."

"What do you have there, Batman?" Poison Ivy asked.

The spider lunged forward and kicked the metal cylinder out of Batman's hand. The small device sailed through the air.

"I got it!" Fred shouted as he made a run for it. He reached up as he got near.

The spider moved in again and kicked the canister away from him.

"I got it!" Daphne said as the canister sailed toward her.

"No you don't," Ivy said as the giant spider charged her. It swatted the can away just before Daphne could catch it.

Velma pointed to the cylinder as it flew toward Shaggy. "You got it, Shaggy?"

Shaggy covered his face with his hands. "Like, I don't want it!"

WHOOSH!

Just then, Scooby-Doo swung in on a long vine. He grabbed the canister of gas before the spider could knock it away again.

Shaggy peeked from between his fingers. "Way to go, Scoob!"

Scooby ducked and dodged attacks from the spider as his vine carried him high into the air. Once he was over Poison Ivy, he let go and landed behind her. Scooby pressed a button on the canister.

POOF!

A cloud of white smoke burst from the can. It completely covered Ivy and Scooby-Doo.

Everyone froze, waiting to see what would happen next.

HA! HA! HA! HA! A sinister laugh came from atop the spider. The smoke cleared and Poison Ivy was still awake.

Ivy laughed louder. "Did you forget that toxins don't work on me?" she asked. "Especially knock-out gas!"

Scooby-Doo's eyes rolled back as he swooned. "Ooh. . ." He slumped over, leaning against the villain.

"Ugh!" she cried. "Get off me!"

That was just the distraction the Dark Knight needed.

WHIP!

The crime fighter flung a Batarang toward Poison Ivy.

The sharp weapon sliced through the branch she was sitting on. The villain screamed as she and Scooby-Doo tumbled from her tall perch.

"Scoob!" Shaggy shouted as he ran to catch his falling friend. Batman sprinted alongside him.

BAM!

Ivy grunted as she hit a log on the way down. By the time the Dark Knight caught her, she was knocked out cold.

Shaggy grunted as he caught his unconscious friend. "Like, don't worry, Scoob," he said. "I got you, pal."

RUMMMMMMBLE!

Everything shook as the spider fell apart, crumbling to the ground.

KRAK! BAM! SMASH!

"Look out!" Fred warned as a giant tree fell in front of them. All the trees began toppling over as huge cracks spider-webbed across the jungle floor.

"What's happening?!" Daphne asked.

"With Ivy knocked out, the entire island is no longer under her control," Velma replied.

"She's right," Batman said. "We have to get out of here before everything sinks back into the ocean."

With Poison Ivy draped over his shoulder, Batman sprinted through the jungle. Fred, Velma, and Daphne were right behind him. Shaggy huffed along as he brought up the rear, carrying the knocked out and very heavy Scooby-Doo.

The group didn't have to worry about any killer plants on the way back. But they did have to dodge more falling trees while leaping over growing cracks in the ground.

By the time they reached the boats, the trees that held them had sunk into the ocean. Both watercraft floated next to a shrinking beach.

Batman hauled Ivy onto his Batboat and strapped her in. Meanwhile, Fred, Velma, and Daphne climbed onto their boat.

Daphne scanned the collapsing island. "Where are Shaggy and Scooby?"

Shaggy stumbled out of the jungle holding Scooby-Doo in his arms. Out of breath, Shaggy dropped to his knees.

"Like, I'm not going to make it," he said. "If it weren't for that knock-out gas . . ."

The Dark Knight shook his head. "That wasn't knock-out gas," he said. "It was just a smoke bomb. I needed a distraction."

Shaggy stared at Batman for a moment. "Well that means . . ." He glanced at Scooby and saw the canine peeking back at him with one open eye.

"Hee-hee-hee-hee-hee-hee," Scooby giggled.

Shaggy's eyes widened. "You big faker!"

Scooby-Doo gave Shaggy's face a big lick before taking off toward the boat.

With newfound energy, Shaggy chased after him. "Come back here, Scooby-Doo!" he yelled.

Scooby giggled again. "Rooby-dooby-doo!"

POISON IVY

Real Name: Pamela Isley

Occupation: Professional Criminal, Botanist

Base: Gotham City

Height: 5 feet 6 inches

Weight: 110 pounds

Eyes: Green

Hair: Red

Powers/Abilities: Unaffected by toxins, able to release harmful scents, and able to control plants with her mind. She is also a skilled martial artist and gymnast, making her a tricky foe to capture.

Biography: Unaffected by plant toxins and poisons since birth, Pamela Isley's love of plants began to grow like a weed at an early age. She eventually became a botanist, or plant scientist. Through reckless experiments with various plant life, Pamela Isley's skin itself became poisonous. Her venomous lips and poisonous plant weapons present a real problem for Batman. But Poison Ivy's most dangerous quality is her extreme love of nature—she cares more about the smallest seedling than any human life.

- Poison Ivy was once engaged to Gotham City's district attorney, Harvey Dent, who eventually became the villain Two-Face! Their relationship ended when Dent built a prison on a field of wildflowers, accidentally earning Ivy's wrath.

- Poison Ivy releases toxic scents that can be harmful to humans. Whenever she is locked up in Arkham Asylum, a wall of Plexiglas must separate her from the guards to ensure their safety.

- Ivy's connection to plants is so strong that she can control them by thought alone! The control she has over her lethal plants makes her a dangerous foe for the police—as well Batman and the rest of the Batman Family.

BIOGRAPHIES

Michael Anthony Steele has been in the entertainment industry for more than 27 years, writing for television, movies, and video games. He has authored more than 120 books for exciting characters and brands including Batman, Superman, Wonder Woman, Spider-Man, Shrek, Scooby-Doo, *WISHBONE*, LEGO City, Garfield, *Night at the Museum*, and *The Penguins of Madagascar.* Steele lives on a ranch in Texas, but he enjoys meeting his readers when he visits schools and libraries all across the country. For more information, visit MichaelAnthonySteele.com.

Dario Brizuela works traditionally and digitally in many different illustration styles. His work can be found in a wide range of properties, including Star Wars Tales, DC Super Friends, Transformers, Scooby-Doo! Team-Up, DC Super Hero Girls, and more. Brizuela lives in Buenos Aires, Argentina.

GLOSSARY

commotion (kuh-MOH-shuhn)—a lot of noisy, excited activity

cylinder (SI-luhn-duhr)—a shape with flat, circular ends and sides shaped like a tube

fossilized (FAH-suhl-eyezd)—preserved as rock

grapnel (GRAP-nuhl)—a grappling hook connected to a rope that can be fired like a gun

passageway (PASS-ij-way)—an alley, hallway, or tunnel that allows you to pass from one place to another

prehistoric (pree-hi-STOR-ik)—from a time before history was recorded

puncture (PUHNGK-chur)—to make a hole with a sharp object

sinister (SIN-uh-stur)—seeming evil and threatening

toxin (TOK-sin)—a poisonous substance produced by a living thing

unconscious (uhn-KON-shuhss)—not awake; not able to see, feel, or think

vegetation (vej-uh-TAY-shuhn)—plant life

THINK ABOUT IT

1. Batman teams up with Scooby-Doo and the Mystery Inc. gang in this story. Do you think the hero could have foiled Poison Ivy's plot without their help? Explain your answer.

2. Scooby and Shaggy disguise themselves as tree monsters to retrieve Batman's Utility Belt. Why was it so important for them to return that piece of equipment to the Dark Knight?

3. Why does Scooby-Doo pretend to get knocked out by the gas he sprays at Poison Ivy? Why does he continue faking it until the very end of the story?

WRITE ABOUT IT

1. Which member of the Mystery Inc. gang is your favorite? Write a paragraph explaining who you like the best and why.

2. Poison Ivy has the power to create giant monsters out of plants. If you had her power, what type of creature would you create? Write a short paragraph describing your plant monster and then draw a picture of it.

3. At the end of the story, Batman places Poison Ivy in the Batboat. What happens next? Write a new chapter describing how he takes her to Arkham Asylum or how she escapes. You decide!

READ THEM ALL!

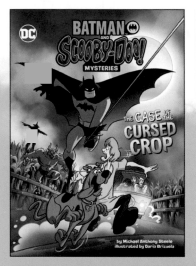

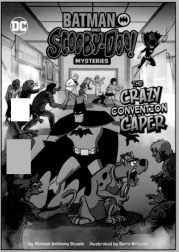